I Love Daddy

Lizi Boyd

CANDLEWICK PRESS
CAMBRIDGE, MASSACHUSETTS

When I'm with Daddy,
I feel big and tall,

and cozy and small,
all in one day.

We have lots of adventures.
"Come on, let's go," says Daddy.

Sometimes things are scary, but
when Daddy's there, I feel brave.

When I peep, "The water's too cold,"
Daddy says, "Try it."

The swimming feels
good once I am wet.

"I'm tired," I peep.
Together we rest in the hammock.

"Why is the sky blue?" I ask.
Daddy tells me. He knows everything.

"Daddy, will you play your whistle?" I peep.

Daddy plays. I tap, tap, tap with sticks
on a log. Together we make music.

Daddy and I fly a kite.
"Hold on tight," says Daddy.

The kite pulls me as it goes higher and higher. Daddy helps me hold the kite.

Daddy shows me how to be kind.
It makes me feel good.

Our neighbor gives us a basket of berries.
Daddy and I say, "Thank you very much."

I help Daddy in the kitchen.

We wash the berries.
Together we make a delicious pie.

We play King on the Rock.

"One more game," says Daddy.

We climb. We giggle. We're all kings.

"What a great day," says Daddy.
"We'll make time to play every day.

I love you."

"I love you too, Daddy."